This Little Tiger book belongs to:

_____

_____

_____

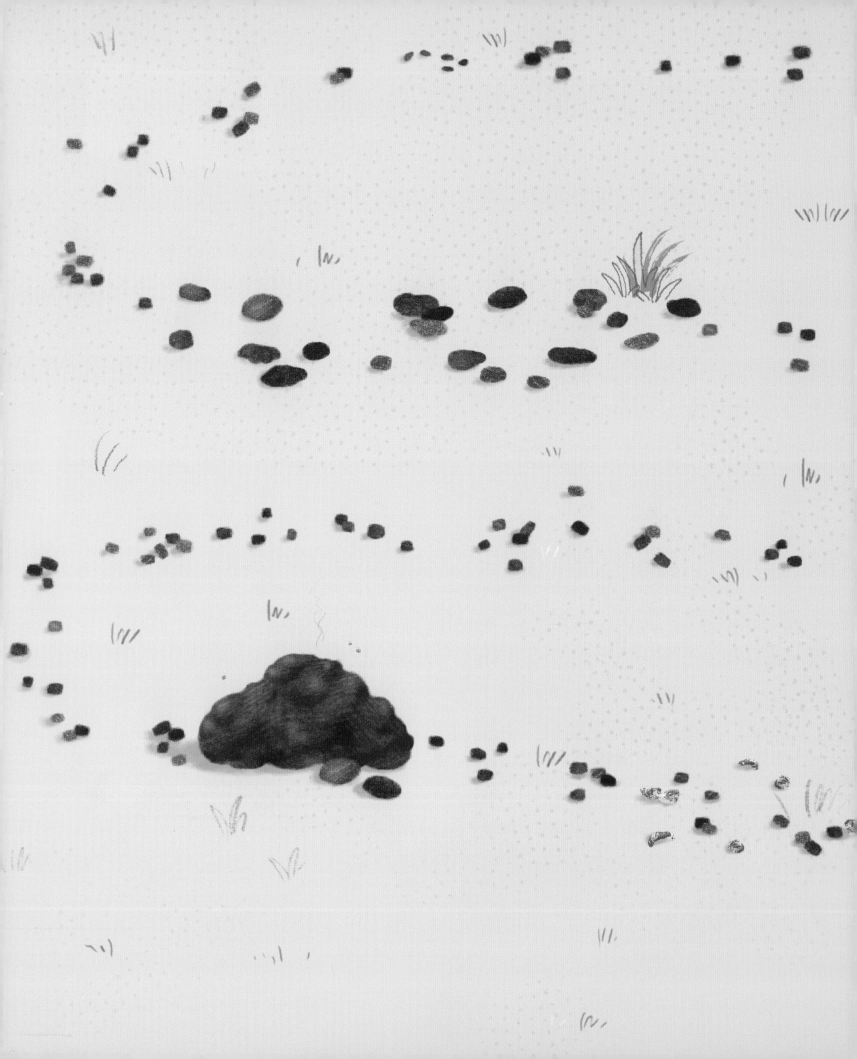

FLAMINGOES

GIANT TORTOISE TURNS 80!

VISIT HIM TODAY

Be Snappy!

VISIT OUR Crocodiles

For Elliott, Scarlet, Gabby, Annie, Matilda, Avery, Henry and Leo, with all my love ~ S S

For the real Arabella ~ A G

LITTLE TIGER PRESS LTD.
an imprint of the Little Tiger Group
1 Coda Studios, 189 Munster Road, London SW6 6AW
Imported into the EEA by Penguin Random House Ireland,
Morrison Chambers, 32 Nassau Street, Dublin D02 YH68
www.littletiger.co.uk

First published in Great Britain 2020

Printed in China * LTP/1400/3914/0321

10 9 8 7 6 5 4

McGREW ZOO

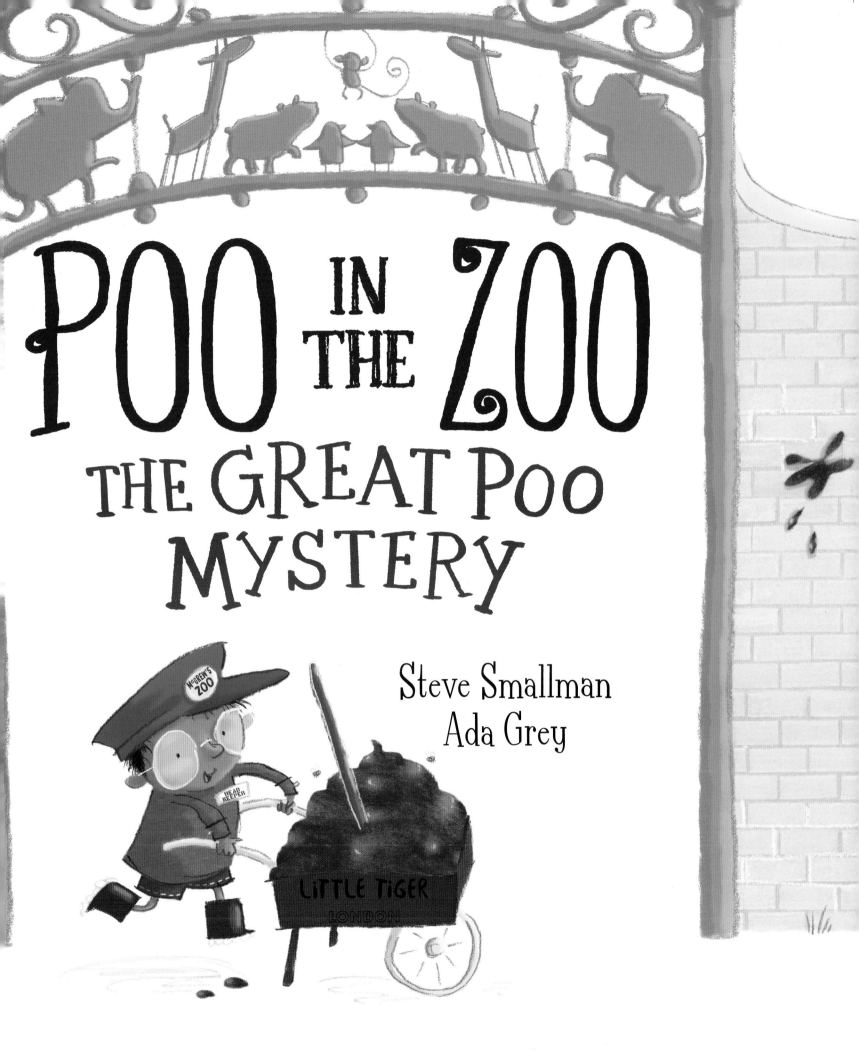

POO IN THE ZOO
THE GREAT POO MYSTERY

Steve Smallman
Ada Grey

LITTLE TIGER
LONDON

Little Bob McGrew was a keeper in the zoo.

He was always very busy, there was **such** a lot to do!

But it didn't bother Bob, as he loved his job,

And his good friend Robbie Robot helped, by picking up the **poo!**

Robbie was unstoppable, anything 'ploppable'
Was cleared with his scoop and his little **poop** hoover.

Fox **poo,**

ox **poo,**

cockatoo or croc **poo** . . .

He really was a pooper scooping, **super Poo** remover!

It was getting quite late,
so Bob closed the gate.

His animals all settled down
and closed their sleepy eyes.

Robbie went to bed in his own cosy shed,

But Chipmunk slept in places that were always a surprise!

Then next day at 8 o'clock, Bob got a nasty shock.

"My zoo is full of POO!" he cried.

"And Robbie's run away!"

ROBBIE'S
SHED

McGREW'S
ZOO

HEAD
KEEPER

Then a lady all in tweed,
who was very strange indeed

Hollered, "Never fear, young zoo keeper! I'm here to save the day!"

"I'm Arabella Slater, I'm a **Poo** Investigator.
Of all the 'number two' detectives I'm the **number one**!

I stopped the Doodoo Doctor in his **poo-poo** helicopter!

Who else could find a **rabbit poo**
inside a currant bun?"

"I found the long-lost **poo**
of the beast of Kathmandu,

I solved the famous phantom
poo-poo flinger mystery,

I'll soon discover who has been '**pooping**' up your zoo,

And I'll find your little **robot**, dearie, just you wait and see!"

Arabella searched for **clues** and she found all sorts of **poos,**

In places that a pile of **poo** should really never be.

Then by Robbie's shed she saw some broken wires on the floor.

She cried out, "Whoopsie-doodoo!" Then she whispered, "Follow me!"

Through the woods so shady went the **speedy, tweedy lady**,

With Bob and all his animals on tippy-toes behind.

They saw some rather **fishy** poos,

some **lumpy** poos,

some **squishy** poos.

They watched their step, and held their breath,
and **wondered** what they'd find.

Then they all heard a **clattering**, some bleeping and 'kersplattering',
And crept into a glade where **Robbie Robot ran amuck!**

He was spinning **round** and round,
spreading **poop** upon the ground.

"Oh no!" yelled Bob.

"His hoover's switched to **blow** instead of **suck!**"

"Stand back!" cried Arabella pulling out a HUGE umbrella.
They all ducked down behind it to avoid a **poo-poo** shower!

But Arabella knew just exactly what to do,

She asked Giraffe to reach across and turn off Robbie's power!

They opened Robbie's chest and they found a tiny nest.

"Look!" called Bob. "It's Chipmunk! And he's chewed through Robbie's wires!"

"I guessed this little fella might be there," said Arabella,

As she quickly mended Robbie with her **poo** detective pliers.

They flicked on Robbie's power, and in less than half an hour,
He'd whizzed around and picked up every single **poop** in sight.

WELCOME to GLOOP'S POO MUSEUM

Arabella said, "Goodbye!" as she zoomed into the sky.

Bob waved then said, "It's time for bed, I'm really . . . pooped! Goodnight!"

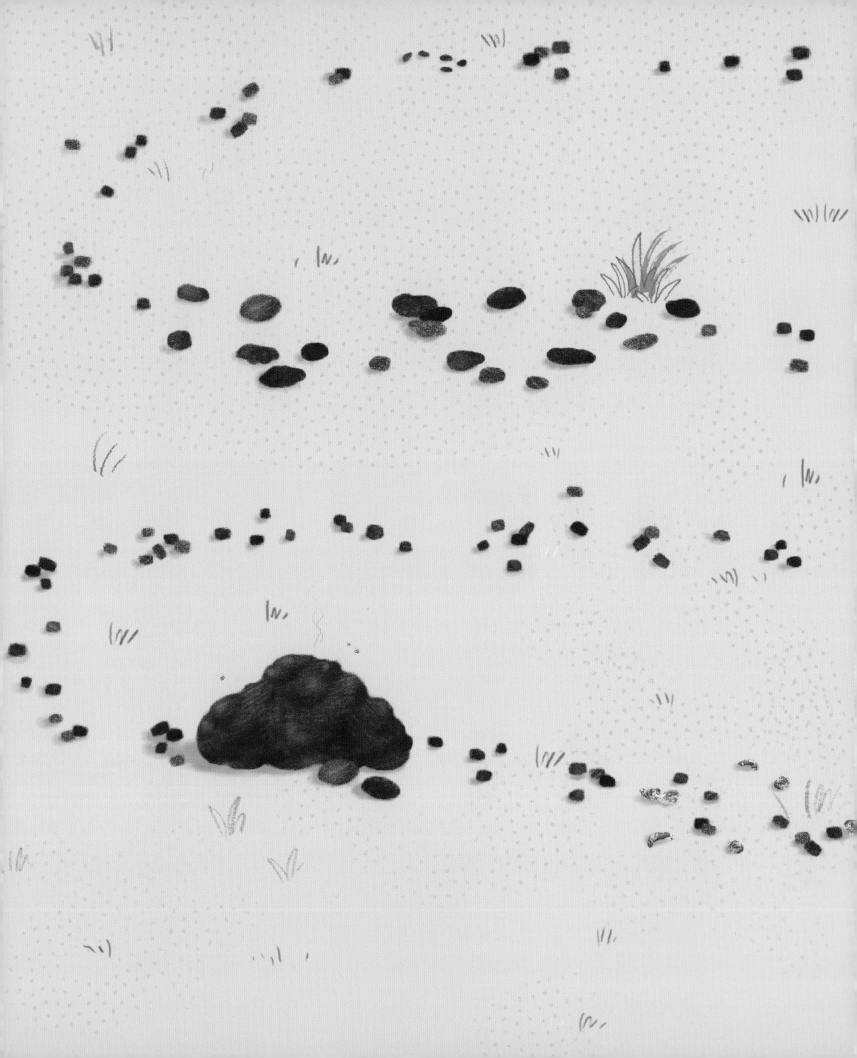

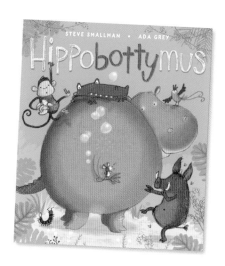

Hippobottymus

STEVE SMALLMAN • ADA GREY

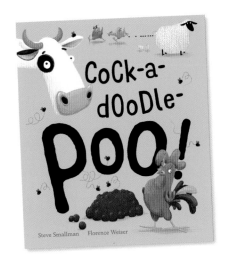

Cock-a-doodle-poo!

Steve Smallman   Florence Weiser

The Monkey with a Bright Blue Bottom

STEVE SMALLMAN   NICK SCHON

Dragon Stew

More fabulously funny stories from Steve Smallman!

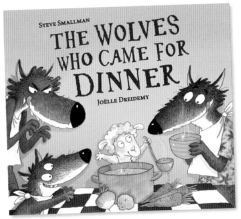

STEVE SMALLMAN

THE WOLVES WHO CAME FOR DINNER

JOËLLE DREIDEMY

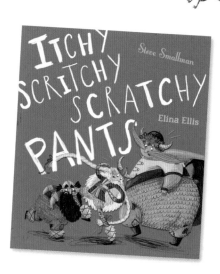

ITCHY SCRITCHY SCRATCHY PANTS

Steve Smallman   Elina Ellis

LITTLE TIGER

For information regarding any of the above titles or for our catalogue, please contact us: Little Tiger Press Ltd, 1 Coda Studios, 189 Munster Road, London SW6 6AW * Tel: 020 7385 6333
E-mail: contact@littletiger.co.uk * www.littletiger.co.uk